10

Short Fairy Tale Stories

Martin B. Flores

10 is about the journey.

When I began writing *10*, I wasn't in the best place in my life. Considering all the obstacles I've faced, what on earth made me write a book?

Even though I've always had a positive mindset and optimism for the future, writing this book made me dig deep into my heart and soul. I just knew I could get through anything that was in my way.

Sometimes, putting the complexities of modern adult life aside and returning to the lessons of childhood is the best way forward. The stories in *10* are accessible to everyone, and what they teach is relevant to all ages and backgrounds.

Writing the final story, *The Way to the Treasure*, reminded me that if you want good things, you must do good things for others. Like Marty, sometimes I did the right thing just because I knew I was supposed to. I've made my share of mistakes, and I haven't always been the man I should be.

Once I understood what this really meant, I started doing good deeds because I wanted to, not because I expected anything in return. I learned that we all face certain obstacles for a reason. I worked on bettering myself, I made up for past mistakes, and kept looking forward.

To those who believed in me, thank you. You are one of the many reasons I wrote this. I hope this book is a reminder, a companion, and a compass for you, and all its readers. The stories contained within will show you that you shouldn't let even the biggest challenges stand in the way of your goals.

Greatness is around the corner.

Contents

Harley and the Black Cat

Since ancient times, it was believed that black cats are very bad luck.

Every time somebody saw a black cat, especially if it crossed their path, they thought they were cursed and would run away in fear.

One particularly sunny day, an adorable little girl named Harley was wandering around her small town. Suddenly, Harley saw a baby black cat meowing sadly by the fountain in the center of town. Harley wondered why nobody had helped this little lost kitten. She gently picked up the cat, which stopped crying straight away and headed for home. When she passed the townspeople, they turned away from her and ran away in fear! Harley wondered what was wrong with everybody.

Harley lived with just her mother because her father died not long ago. She thought about how much she missed him as she carried the kitten home. Harley accidentally slammed the door entering the house; her mom whipped her head around to yell at her about it and, in shock at the sight of the black cat, instead yelled, "Why did you bring a black cat to the house? Black cats are bad luck!"

Harley said, "This cat needed my help, and I want to keep it."

Not pleased, Mom gave the order, "You have a week to get rid of it."

Harley was sad, knowing she had to let go of her new best

friend in a week. She shook her head and walked away. She just didn't understand why everyone thinks black cats are bad luck!

In the meantime, Harley would cherish her time with the shiny black cat, even though it was only for a week.

A couple of days passed, and Harley was playing with the black cat. Harley told her mom, "I don't think this cat is bad luck, Mommy. Nothing bad has happened."

All her mother said was, "You have five more days to keep the cat."

Another couple of days went by, and still, nothing bad had happened. Everything seemed normal. Harley, with the cat nestled in her arms, came up to her mom while she was cooking dinner and begged her, "Can we please keep the cat? Nothing bad will happen!"

Harley, petting the cat, hoped it was putting on its sweet face for her mother. Mom, a little frustrated to be put in this position, turned back to her cooking, and just said, "No!"

The next day, Harley's mom had to go to work and, because she had nobody to stay with Harley, she had to take Harley and the cat to work with her. Harley's mom was a little scared of what people would think of her for letting her daughter have a black cat, as she knew they lived in a very superstitious town. She was right, of course. All of her co-workers stared at her, Harley, and the black cat with disapproval and fear.

Nonetheless, Harley cherished her time with the beautiful black cat. While Mom was working, the boss showed up and asked her, "Have you seen a baby black cat?" Over the mom's shoulder, her boss saw Harley playing with the cat and said, "That's my black cat. Where did you find it?"

Harley was afraid of the boss and said so quietly he could barely hear her, "I found it wandering around town. It was crying."

Happy to have his black cat back, the boss decided to

reward Harley's mom with a week's paid vacation for taking such good care of the cat, although little did the boss know that it was Harley that took care of the kitten!

Mom beamed at Harley, "You were right, sweetie. This black cat isn't bad luck at all. It's good luck."

Harley smiled, "I told you so." The cat purred, its jet-black tail flicked happily, and it seemed to smile too.

Later, her mom gave Harley a big hug. "You taught me a valuable lesson. One shouldn't believe something just because everyone else does. You have to follow your heart."

The boss realized how close Harley was with his black cat and he decided to let Harley keep it. Harley and her mom were thrilled!

From then on, the black cat brought only good luck to Harley and her mom. It brought so much good luck that her mom shared her good fortune with the town and before long, everybody changed their minds about black cats. It was no longer a town of superstition!

King David

In a far distant land, in a great kingdom, lived a King named David. King David married a lovely Queen, and the blessed day came when a lovely male child, named Arthur, was born. Sadly, the Queen passed away during childbirth.

King David never remarried because his love for the Queen was so great, and he could never love another. As

Arthur grew, the King realized he was just too sweet-natured to be his heir to the throne and that he wouldn't be a strong leader. Arthur also didn't seem to care about such things. So, the King began a thoughtful search for the perfect woman for Arthur to marry, as he was anxious to have an heir to the throne. (Great Kings plan ahead.)

Eventually, the King found a very lovely and sweet Princess for Arthur to marry, and they had a grand and beautiful wedding. A year and a half passed, and King David summoned his son to ask, "Why hasn't a child been born yet?" The King warned Arthur that if no child was born within the year, he would have to leave the Princess and marry someone who would bear the King an heir.

Unbeknownst to King David and Arthur, the Princess was listening behind a curtain, and she approached Arthur about it that evening.

To Arthur's surprise, she agreed with the King. "Arthur, your father is right. Although I love you with an undying love, I must release you if we can't have a child. It's for the good of the kingdom. Your father is getting old, and a child must be born."

Later, the Princess went to the chapel's altar and lit candles. She prayed to the Good Spirit, to the Fairies and the Angels to send her a child, so she could stay married to her beloved Arthur. The Fairies appeared and told her the good news! Her child would be kind and help all the people in the kingdom. The Princess was so happy – and relieved!

True to the Fairies word, within the year, the Princess had a child. There was only one problem. The baby was a girl – – whom they named Helen. They knew the King would be disappointed because of his insistence that a boy inherit his throne. Sure enough, King David pronounced, "A girl cannot be an heir to the throne!" Arthur told his father not to worry, that a boy would be born later.

Unfortunately, after two years, no other children were born, boy or girl! The King again approached his son and told him that he still wanted a male heir and, if it didn't happen soon, Arthur would have to divorce the Princess. Arthur said, "No, I'm not going to divorce her. I love my wife." The King was really upset and stormed off.

Seven years passed by all too quickly, and for all of those years, the King wasn't happy with the Princess or with his only grandchild, Helen, whom he sadly ignored as if she didn't exist. The only reason he didn't kick them both out of the kingdom was because he knew he would lose his son in the process.

One day, the King was playing chess with one of his friends. His friend stood up to leave. "We'll finish this later."

Helen, eight years old at the time, tiptoed into the room where the King had been playing chess. Helen asked the King, "Are you my grandfather?"

The King didn't say anything, so the girl asked a little louder, "Are you my grandfather?"

Still no answer. There was a bowl of candy on the table,

and Helen sweetly asked the King if she could please have a piece of candy. The King said gruffly, "Only one." The King rang for one of his servants to take Helen back to her mom and dad.

Moments later, the child returned, and the King asked, "What do you want now?"

Helen said, "It's about your chess game, Grandfather. It's all wrong. You won't win that way."

The King squinted at her, "What do you know about chess? Did your mother send you?" Helen just smiled.

When the King called for the servant to take Helen away, the Princess came instead. The King turned to Helen and said, "You're staying with me." This frightened the Princess. Why would King David suddenly want Helen to stay? She reluctantly left her daughter with the King for the day, where Helen advised him on chess and other matters we will never know about.

Later, King David was in serious talks with his war advisor about going to war with a neighboring country. When the advisor left, Helen walked up behind the King and glanced at the plans. She shook her little head and told the King, "You won't win the war that way. You must attack from the rear, then head up to the front."

The King asked Helen, "What do you know about war?"

She smiled. "We will win the war and I'll be by your side." The King checked with his war advisor and told him exactly what Helen told him about the war plans.

The advisor told the King, "She's right! This is a perfect plan to win the war. Why didn't I think of it myself?"

As time went on, the King realized his granddaughter was wise beyond her years, and he basked in the love she gave him. He became quite attached to Helen and was really happy with her by his side. As she promised, they did win the war.

At just the right time, the King declared that Helen would be the rightful heir to his throne and, when he died peacefully in his sleep one night, Helen took over the throne of King David to become Queen Helen.

The Apple and the Pot Maker

In an old ancient land, there was a great kingdom with no heir to the throne. It was foretold that there would be a savior for the land. As ancient as the land was, there was an equally ancient apple tree in the vast garden of the castle. Over the past several years, the tree became old and started decaying.

In spite of its decay, a beautiful shiny red apple hung from the very top of the tree, year after year, in summer and even in winter. According to legend, whoever was able to bring down the apple would marry the Princess and save the kingdom.

Along came a pot maker named Oscar. Oscar was a good craftsman and also had a lovely daughter named Olga. Oscar and Olga walked down a long road towards the back of the castle, where they discovered the kingdom's kitchen. Oscar asked the chef, "Do any pots need to be repaired or made?"

The chef said, "Yes." The chef asked, "Are you Oscar, the pot maker?"

Oscar replied, "Yes, I am."

The chef said, "We have heard of you and that you're really good at what you do." Oscar blushed, for he was a humble man.

Oscar began to work, but he found it really difficult to fix or make the pots, so he had to be devoted to his work and stay focused on it. While Oscar worked away, Olga wandered around the gardens outside of the kitchen. She looked up and saw the shining red apple on top of the ancient tree. The apple was really beautiful, and Olga couldn't stop looking at it. She was mesmerized by it! She went back to her father and kept telling him about the apple, even though it was obvious he was very busy working! Oscar couldn't concentrate on his work and, in exasperation, said, "Daughter, please, I have no time. I will buy anything you want after I'm done." Olga kept crying to her father about the beautiful shining apple on the tree – you'd think she was a child!

After many interruptions, Oscar grabbed a stone out of frustration and threw it in the direction of the apple. He miraculously hit the apple, which promptly fell with a thud from the tree. So many had tried to take down the apple, but all had failed.

As soon as the apple hit the ground, Oscar heard a blur of sounds: trumpets, drums, running horses, and men who immediately surrounded him. The men asked him, "Who took down the apple?"

With a shaky voice, Oscar said "I did." Oscar tried to explain that his daughter interrupted his work, and he apologized for dropping the apple out of anger. He added that he would pay a reasonable amount for it. At that moment, they took Oscar and his daughter before the King. Oscar wondered why knocking down a stupid apple was such a big deal for him to have to face the King!

The King sat on his royal throne and spoke, shocking Oscar to his core said, "You must marry my daughter because you are now the savior of our kingdom." Oscar wondered if he was joking! "But I am married already, sir, I mean sire, your highness, sir." Oscar was very nervous. "I just cannot do that."

The King said, "You will, pot maker! I set the laws, and your wife and children are being taken away as I speak! As of today, you will live in this kingdom and marry my daughter." Within five days, Oscar married the young and beautiful Princess, but he was clearly not a happy groom.

Unfortunately, after spending time together, Oscar realized

that he wasn't romantically interested in his new wife. He slept on the couch in their royal suite, if you get the picture! Oscar felt he must remain loyal to his wife and children, whom he prayed every day to be reunited with. As one day after the other passed by, all Oscar could do was cry big tears and long to be with his wife and children. On top of it, he barely ate anything. When the Princess spoke to Oscar, he responded as little as possible. The Princess wasn't happy either.

Oscar said to himself, "If I ever see Olga again, I will give her the biggest spanking for causing me so much trouble," although he really loved her dearly and missed her.

One day in the great hall, a message arrived of great danger! The most feared army in the world was about to invade the kingdom! The King, troubled by the news, asked his advisors and soldiers, "Who will go to face this army?" Of course, not one of them replied because of the army's fierce reputation! Oscar, however, heard the news and said to himself, "Better to face the army and death than to live in such sadness." He went before the King and told him that he wanted to face this powerful army. The King was amazed by this and was very grateful. He told his soldiers that they were now under Oscar's command, and he ordered them to do exactly what Oscar said... and did... or face the firing squad!

Oscar, being a wanderer his whole life, knew what he needed for the long trip. He found the best horse in the kingdom, which was the King's horse. Commands were that everyone trade in their old, tired horses for new, strong ones.

Oscar gathered his supplies: fat pieces of bacon, meat, coffee, sugar, some dough to fry bread, a pot to cook in, and some blankets. All the soldiers did the exact same thing. Oscar's new army rode away from the castle in the direction of the invading army. Oscar and his army came to a beautiful open field, and he said to himself, "This would be a beautiful place to camp with my wife and children."

They set up camp for the night, and in the morning, they

moved out to find the imposing army. Oscar cut off a little branch to gently tap his horse. Oscar's army did the same thing. They came to a huge river and there was no way for them to get across. Out of anger, Oscar threw the branch into the river. Likewise, the army did the same, which turned out to be a good thing! All the branches piled up on top of each other, creating a dam.

They were now able to cross the river. Oscar and his army went to higher ground to set up a camp. All the men, including Oscar, were tired and hungry, so they prepared to make a meal. They smoked meat on the fire pit they built and used a stick to turn their meat around, like a rotisserie.

Unbeknownst to Oscar and his army, the enemy was camping nearby. Oscar reminded his men that the opposing army was the fiercest in the land and they had never lost a war. Oscar and his men were trying to hide their fear! The enemy army sent out spies to scout Oscar's army. They sent along a highly trained war dog as well. Not that well trained, though, because the dog smelled Oscar's meat, crashed wildly through the bushes, and snatched the meat. Oscar was so upset that he started chasing after the dog and screaming.

All of a sudden, all of Oscar's army was chasing this one poor war dog, screaming and waving their swords in their hands! It was a sight to behold!

The spy, watching everything from the bushes, returned to the leader of his army with a report. "Let's leave this land! They're chasing one dog and screaming! They're maniacs!" Out of fear, the enemy army packed up quickly and rode out of the kingdom.

Oscar and his army returned with a great victory, having saved the kingdom after all!

The happy King draped his arm around Oscar's shoulder. "Whatever you wish upon I'll give it to you." Oscar looked sincerely into the King's eyes and said, not at all nervous anymore, "I wish to be reunited with my wife and my children and given freedom to leave."

The King said, "It shall be done."

The King knew that was what Oscar wanted more than anything, so he nodded his head for the guard to open the huge double doors.

Oscar's wife and children rushed in and surrounded Oscar with hugs and kisses! Oscar winked at Olga. Oscar, the pot maker, was now the happiest man in the world.

The Governor Who Loved Horses

There was a handsome and charming young man named John, who was born into a very rich family. His father, Henry, owned the biggest ranch in the state, where he bred champion racehorses. John learned to ride before he could walk. Even his first word, which was "faster", was said to his pony.

When John turned 25 years old and finished college, he went into politics. He was very popular, and it wasn't long before he became the Governor.

John married a beautiful woman named Barbara. Barbara, having had many suitors, thought she was the luckiest woman in the world, marrying a handsome politician who owned such amazing horses.

As time went on, they had three beautiful children: twin girls and a boy, John Jr. The family lived in the grand and stately Governor's mansion with many servants to help them. When photographers came to the mansion to take their picture for the Sunday magazine, they were the picture-perfect family!

As time went on, John spent less and less time with his family and more and more time with his horses.

Sometimes he didn't come home from the ranch to sleep. Barbara started to think that maybe he loved his horses more than his wife and children.

Years passed by. As his children were growing up, he

missed most of their birthday parties. When his son got engaged, he wasn't there. He didn't show up for their anniversaries, and, eventually, Barbara stopped expecting him to.

If he wasn't busy being the Governor, he was with his horses. He took his horses, instead of his family, on vacation. They rode through gorgeous mountains out West.

One day his wife asked him, "Do you know that your son got engaged? Do you know that one of your daughters went away to college and the other daughter got married? Your children don't even know you anymore; they wouldn't recognize you if you walked past them. One day you're going to find us gone." It was not the first time she said this, but John just did not seem to hear. If only Barbara spoke horse language…

Out of the blue, John got a call that his prized horse was having a baby horse. By coincidence, his daughter was expecting her baby that same night. Immediately, John left to go to the ranch.

His wife already knew she had to leave him. She'd known for a long time.

When John returned from the ranch, his wife and family were gone. John handed out blue cigars for the birth of the colt.

The King Against Himself

Once upon a time, there was a King who had it all. His castle was the biggest in the land. The King was the happiest man alive, and there wasn't anything that could ruin his perfect life.

Even though he knew he had a wonderful life and didn't need anything, the King woke up one day wanting more. Day by day, he grew more and more selfish. He even forced his servants to work twice as hard.

The King wanted a bigger castle, a bigger kingdom, and greater riches. His obsession for wanting more continued to grow. The King began yelling at the servants, even though they were doing their job as well as they always did. The servants, little by little, grew tired of the King's mean behavior.

When the day came to reward the servants for all of their hard work, instead of rewarding them with the pay they deserved, he gave the servants less than what he usually paid them. The servants were shocked! To make matters worse, the King screamed at all the servants, "Now, get back to work! No more rest!"

The King got completely lost in his selfish greedy mind and he continued to treat the servants with no respect. As time went on, the servants, little by little, stopped doing their jobs. The King yelled and yelled at the servants to work, or they would be punished. The servants ignored the King's orders, gathered together in one big group and started discussing what to do about the mean King.

The leader of the servants said, "I'm tired of how the King is treating us. We don't deserve this! Let's stop working for the King altogether and go to a village not far from here."

The King approached the leader of the servants and demanded, "What is the meaning of this? Why aren't you guys working? I am your King!"

The leader told the King, "I don't know what's gotten into you, but you´re not treating us right. For that, we're going to leave this kingdom."

The King, in complete astonishment, watched as his former servants walked down the road and away from his kingdom. The King, left alone, wandered sadly around his kingdom. He realized, with nobody helping him grow his kingdom and with nobody to share his castle with, his wealth didn't mean much to him anymore.

As the months passed, the King became miserable with nobody to help run the kingdom. He also realized that there was no kingdom with nobody else around. As he pondered about this, the King asked himself, "Where did it all go wrong?"

Little by little, he started to realize that treating his servants disrespectfully and not giving them the rewards they deserved just pushed them away. It was all his fault! The King didn't feel much like a King anymore. Even though he had so much wealth, it didn't mean much to him without sharing it.

One day, the King began thinking of a way to get his kingdom back. He tried to think of how he might make his servants happy, and he decided to do something he'd never done before. He decided to go over to the village where the servants were. Even though the servants weren't happy with the pay they were getting working at the other village, at least they were being treated right.

The servants were surprised to see their King arrive. They gathered tightly together in a group, expecting the worst. The leader of the servants approached the King and asked (not too nicely), "What are you doing here?"

The King then really surprised everyone! Head hung down in shame, he actually apologized to the servants about how badly he treated them. The King pronounced, "I would like all of you to come back to my kingdom. If you do, I promise to treat you right and pay all of you handsomely. As a matter of fact, I would like to share half of my wealth with all of you! Without you guys, I am no King."

The servants, in complete amazement, eagerly agreed to go back to the kingdom where they were once so happy.

This time around, however, the King was happier than ever knowing he had his kingdom back and his friends around, for even though they were his servants, the King now thought of them as his friends.

The King's wealth now meant a lot more to him knowing that he was sharing it.

The Lost Horses

A young and peppy man named Austin lived in the middle of the Midwest with his petite and pretty wife, Joanne. Over time, they had two precious and playful sons, Alex and David. They lived on a very small horse ranch, surrounded by dense forest, which provided them a simple, but happy, life.

That is, until Joanne got a bad cold that got progressively worse. They learned, too late, that she had pneumonia. She died peacefully with Austin and the boys holding her hand. Austin was devastated because he loved her very much.

Faced with raising the boys on his own, he decided to get the boys an Australian sheepdog, even though there were no sheep. The boys named the dog Rusty because of his rust-colored patches. He also had one blue eye and one brown, which they thought was very funny. Although the dog made the boys very happy, they still missed their mother.

Austin, who made his living buying, breeding, and selling horses, hired a few cowboys to help out. The horses roamed the green pastures in the summer but stayed in the barn during the harsh winters. Austin had a big dream. One day he decided to go for it. He invested his entire life savings in buying two amazing black Arabian stallions from the Middle East. When the horses arrived at the ranch, he was one happy man; his dream was fulfilled.

The family was handling the loss of Joanne as best as they could, although Alex tended to get into a bit more trouble during this time, which sometimes happens when kids lose their mothers too soon.

One day, Austin found cigarettes and matches in Alex's jeans. All "heck" broke loose, and Dad grounded Alex. He had to come straight home every day after school for a month! Alex yelled at him, "The cowboys all smoke – why can't I?" He stormed off to his room and slammed the door. Austin looked up into space. "Joanne, I miss you."

As you know, winters in the Midwest can be brutal, especially for animals living in a barn. Austin was working hard to fix the broken barn heater before winter set in, but the bitter cold arrived before the replacement parts. To make matters worse, a blinding blizzard soon followed. On the second day of the blizzard, one of the cowboys accidentally left the barn door open. You'd think a cowboy would know better!

That night, the freezing black stallions walked right out of the barn, hoping to find a place to be warm. When Austin trudged into the barn in the dark dawn, he saw that his stallions were gone! His dream and his savings were lost in a heartbeat.

Alex, now nine, and David, eight, heard the commotion outside and woke up. They listened as the cowboys frantically yelled through the fierce wind that the stallions were missing. Without their father realizing, Alex decided that he and David would take Rusty and search for the stallions in the blizzard. Maybe his father wouldn't stay mad at him if he found the horses?

When Austin found out that his sons were gone too, he fell to his knees and cried, "Joanne! Joanne! Joanne!"

In short order, Austin, his cowboys, and several worried neighbors went searching for his sons. Meanwhile, the boys trudged through snowdrifts, sometimes losing each other in the forest. It snowed so hard and fast their boot prints were covered by snow in minutes.

Eventually, the boys found the stallions huddled under

some trees over a mile away. Alex led the horses into a small but cozy cave nearby. Alex started a small fire with some dried twigs and a pack of matches he wasn't supposed to have, but it proved to be a good thing he did! Austin and the searchers kept calling the boys' names through the wind and the blinding snow.

The children couldn't hear them calling – all they could hear was the wailing wind, which sounded a lot like the Banshee! Very scary. The hours passed slowly, and darkness set in. Alex was afraid, but he couldn't let David know it. He didn't really know where they were or how to get home, especially in a blinding blizzard, and he wasn't confident his father would ever find this hidden cave. So they just stayed quietly in the cave with the horses, who seemed to like the warm fire quite a bit.

Austin and the neighbors refused to give up. They now walked through the snow filled forest with lit torches zigzagging through the trees, calling and calling the boys' names.

Suddenly, in the cave quite a ways away, Rusty's ears pricked up, and he began to run around in circles, barking wildly. Austin started yelling at Rusty to be quiet because the horses were getting spooked!

"Rusty! Quiet! Rusty! Rusty!" Rusty just ran out of the cave as fast as he could.

Austin turned to David, "Now we lost our dog!"

Austin almost fell over as Rusty burst through the trees and ran circles around him. Austin realized he was trying to say something, so he followed Rusty back to the cave where he found his sons. The horses and the children were fine. And Alex was right! His father hugged him with tears in his eyes and apologized for being so hard on him. Even though Dad didn't ever want him to smoke, Alex was no longer grounded.

On the way back home, Austin heard a rustle in the trees. He looked behind him and saw the image of his smiling wife, Joanne, blowing him a last kiss.

The Lost Princess

In a country called Russia, there lived a King named Dimitri. His twenty-year-old, charming son, Peter, married the beautiful Princess Lucette from France.

Not too long after, Princess Mara was born. Mara was an exquisitely beautiful baby, with the exception of a wee butterfly shaped birthmark on her right shoulder, which secretly embarrassed Princess Lucette. Sadly, Mara's mother died when she was only two years old.

Prince Peter hired a Nanny named Nancy to take care of Mara because he was so busy being the Prince, he knew he couldn't raise her without help.

Nanny Nancy loved the little Princess, would tell her stories about fairies and knights in shining armor, and gave Princess Mara the nickname, Sweet Fairy.

One early morning, when Princess Mara was three years old and her Nanny Nancy was in the closet looking for a special dress for the day, Mara wandered away, as children tend to do. Climbing down stairways and opening random doors, Princess Mara found a secret passageway. Curious, she followed the long and dark passageway toward the light at the end. When she emerged, she had no idea where she was, but it was definitely outside the castle walls.

As she wandered farther and farther away from the castle, a group of traveling gypsies found her. These people were artisans, pot makers, musicians, and healers. The castle folk considered gypsies grubby and wild, but in fact, they all had kind souls and loved children. When they found the child, she was very dirty and looked lost. They asked her where she was from and, when she said, "I'm a fairy Princess from the castle," they all just laughed and thought she had quite an imagination. They certainly didn't believe that this dingy child was from the castle! Maybe if she had been dressed in one of her finest Princess dresses instead of very plain pajamas, they might have believed her. Instead, they assumed her parents were dead, and she was just a poor abandoned orphan.

The gypsies took the child back with them to their village to raise as their own. By a magical coincidence, they gave her the name Mara as well. The gypsies loved Mara very much, and they knew that she was an exceptionally beautiful and sweet child.

The years passed happily, and her family was celebrating her sixteenth birthday with a gypsy party in the town square. There's nothing like a gypsy party! Mara was happy because her mother had allowed her to wear her first strapless dress for her birthday!

Suddenly, some soldiers rode into the square. The captain of the men approached Mara, "We will rest here. By chance, would you have food and water for my regiment?"

It had been a long journey and the girl, being a kind soul, gave the soldiers some of the food being set up for her birthday celebration, along with cool well water.

As fate would have it, the captain had been a personal bodyguard when Princess Mara was a child. He recognized the birthmark on her right shoulder and jumped up excitedly and told the gypsy family, "This is the long-lost Princess Mara! You must stay here until I return. There is a great reward for you."

The family thought the captain must be crazy, and they went back to celebrating Mara's birthday as if nothing had happened. The butterflies in Mara's stomach told her it was true, but she didn't want to hurt her family celebrating her birthday, so she pretended nothing had happened too.

The captain returned to the kingdom and ran through the castle to find King Dimitri, who was holding forth a very important meeting. The captain, breathless from exertion and excitement, interrupted the meeting as he tried to tell the King that he thought he had seen Princess Mara living with a bunch of gypsies. The King was overwhelmed with emotion. Could it be true? He told the captain, "Go and bring the Princess and her gypsy family before me with all haste."

Riding speedily, the captain arrived back at the tail end of the birthday celebration. He explained to Mara's gypsy family that he believed she was the long-lost Princess, proven by the butterfly birthmark he could plainly see above her strapless dress. He said that the King was offering a handsome reward for her return if it was confirmed to be true.

The family reacted as you would expect. They were happy their beautiful and sweet daughter might really be a Princess and would be reunited with her rightful father, the King, but were also very sad indeed at the thought of losing her. It's what one calls a mixed blessing.

When the captain returned to the castle with Princess Mara and her adopted family, King Dimitri summoned Nanny Nancy to confirm the birthmark. The nanny, a bit scandalized that the girl was wearing a strapless dress, nevertheless looked long and hard at the butterfly birthmark, now larger than she remembers. She stood up and looked directly at the King. "Your Highness, I confirm that this is the long-lost Princess, Mara. Besides the butterfly birthmark, can you not also see the strong physical resemblance to you, sire?"

The King was so happy that he wept, and so did everyone at the court. Mara also shed a tear. The King opened his arms, and Princess Mara ran into them.

After a moment, the King turned to Mara's gypsy family, who stood awkwardly nearby, and asked, "How did you find my daughter?"

The adopted family explained the story and how they thought that her parents were dead. The King asked the Princess, "How was your life with them?"

Mara cried bittersweet tears and said, "They were wonderful parents to me, and I love them."

The King rewarded Mara's adopted family handsomely, proclaimed them citizens of Russia, and embraced them. The King also gave them a quaint cottage and some land close to the castle, so that they were free to come and go to see Mara for the rest of their lives, which they did.

Happily, ever after comes to mind.

The Pot That's Never Empty

In a far off land, in the distant past, a traveling peddler named Paul trekked through the hot sands of the desert with his caravan of horses and camels. With his devoted wife and six children by his side, Paul sold coffee, tea, spices, sugar, tapestries, and other goods across deserts and plains to tent towns and bigger cities. It was a nomadic but happy life.

Often, the traveling merchants and their families gathered together to camp out and sleep under the stars. The next day they would continue on their journeys.

One blindingly hot day, an older man with piercing eyes, traveling with a quiet and frail child, stopped Paul and his family and asked, "how long before we get to the main city?"

"Sometime tomorrow," Paul said. "Would you and your child like to find some shade and eat with us?" The old man was grateful for the invitation.

Paul looked into his worn black pot and realized there was barely any food, and his family would likely go hungry, but he graciously poured the contents into the bowls of the hungry child and kindly gentlemen.

His wife whispered harshly, "You are always feeding strangers!"

Paul replied, "Be quiet, my anxious wife, for we are blessed."

After enjoying their meal and sharing in heartfelt conversation, the old gentleman bade farewell to Paul and his family. He walked away, hand in hand, with the child. Paul watched as the heat vapors from the setting sun on the desert sand created the illusion of them disappearing.

Later, Paul went to clean the empty pot, but, to his surprise, the pot wasn't empty at all! It was filled to the brim with tender meat and vegetables! Paul turned to his wife and said, "There is food in this pot. How could this be?"

His wife said, "It's not possible! There was no food for the family." They shook their heads in disbelief.

This went on for months. The pot was never empty. Paul was always able to feed his family, as well as the entire caravan, who now held Paul in high esteem.

It turned out that the child and the older gentleman were angels! When they saw that Paul was so kind as to share his food with them, the angels left Paul with the blessing that his pot would never be empty. It was a blessing indeed.

Word spread over all the land that there was a pot that was never empty. When the King of the land heard the fantastic tale, he ordered his soldiers to find the man and bring him and his family and all of their belongings to the King's palace.

When Paul arrived, he was brought before the King on his throne. Because he was a poor man and unsure of the King's laws, he shook from fright as he said to the King, "Sire, why have you brought us here? We didn't break any laws."

The King replied, "I understand that you have put some type of sorcery or witchcraft on a simple black pot, and you are feeding hundreds of people with a boundless supply of food. I must see this for myself. But I warn you: if this is witchcraft or sorcery, you will be harshly punished."

The King led Paul into the courtyard, where the empty pot sat over a fire pit. He commanded Paul to cook a meal of beef and potatoes, which he did as fast as he could. A seemingly endless line of the King's soldiers ate first, and then the King turned to Paul, "It's my turn now. Serve me my plate."

Paul reached into the pot to prepare the King's plate, but to his great surprise, the pot was empty! This didn't look good for Paul at all. The King wasn't happy.

"Why is there no food for me?"

Paul said quietly, "I do not know, my lord."

Embarrassed to be seen this way, the King demanded, "I want an explanation for this. This must be sorcery!"

One of the soldiers, thinking quickly, said to the King, "Oh great King, there is so much food that you can eat, better food than this."

The King, still angry, yelled, "I want this food from this pot!"

The soldier tried again, "You have no need for this, my lord. You are not poor or hungry and will always have the riches of the kingdom at your disposal."

The King didn't look entirely convinced. Paul's very life was on the line. If the King thought this was sorcery, Paul could be jailed, or worse, hung. His anxious wife looked on, more anxious than ever. A worried Paul looked toward heaven and, lips moving quietly, said a quick prayer to his angels.

Just then, the King turned to Paul and said, "I was going to punish you for this, but I believe you are truly a good man. I apologize for doubting you and, instead, I shall reward you. You and your wife and children will live in the kingdom and have everything you need. I do insist, though, that every day you will sit in the center of the city, with the pot that's never empty, and feed those that are in need."

Suddenly, the pot started swinging from side to side, in ever large swings, as if to show that the angels had heard the news and were happy!

Paul felt truly blessed, and the King was happy.

The Wizard

Once upon a time, there was a wise wizard, Wilfred, who lived in a tiny, thatched house in a wee village near the sea. People in that small village were happy and carefree.

When anything did go wrong, they just walked to the sea to visit the wizard for help. The wizard's job was to make sure that everybody in the village stayed healthy and happy. Everything was going smoothly, and Wizard Willy, (he was called Willy by his friends) was doing a fine job.

That is, until one day, another wizard decided to live in that small village. He just rode right up the road with his skinny donkey pulling a bumpy cart filled with bottles of strange and colorful tonics and potions, and even stranger masks from who knows where!

At first, the villagers wouldn't go near the strange wizard, but the quiet-as-a-mouse, Widow Worthy, decided she'd go to him for her rheumatism. She drank the dark potion he gave her and the next day she was laughing and skipping down the road yelling, "I'm young and I'm free, look at me!" Everyone did.

Soon there was a line outside the new wizard's door. People started thinking that two wizards would make the town a better place.

Little did they know, this new wizard was not what he appeared to be.

Meanwhile, Wizard Willy couldn't help but notice he saw fewer and fewer people. Something was up. One dark moonless night, Willy snuck over to the new wizard's cottage and peered through the window. He didn't like what he saw one bit, and he rushed away as fast as he could run in wizard robes!

Wizard Willy knew the new "good" wizard was up to no good, but little did he know that the new wizard was a witch. Technically, he was a warlock, but witch sounds better!

The witch's plan was to deceive people and promise them a better life than the wizard could, but that wasn't the case at all. His plan was to turn that small village evil with bad spells and special potions. He would use that evil power to control everybody.

As the days passed, all you would hear was people arguing with each other and not being nice to one another. There were even a few fist fights! The wizard knew he had to do something, so he decided to use his abilities to try and fix this. Some of the people in the village were still on the good side of things and tried to figure out what was going on with everybody else.

So, the wizard assembled all the people that weren't affected by the evil spells in his cottage. He told them to gather together in a tight circle, with their arms around each other's waists, so he could feel their positive energy. Once the energy reached maximum positive, the wizard would use his abilities and that positive energy to take away the bad spell that was affecting the village. The people did as they were told, closing their eyes, and thinking of their favorite places to be in their life (this makes good energy, by the way!). Some thought of beautiful lakes, while others thought of mountains, or fishing, or the kitchen where they grew up, with sweet smells and a loving mother.

The witch immediately sensed something happening, and he knew he needed to fight the waves of light that were coming over the cottages and through the woods right at him. He needed to fight with as much negative energy as he's ever used.

He quickly called all the people still affected by his bad spells to come to his cottage. He hit them each on the head hard, trying to tap into their bad energy. Everyone stood rubbing their heads in confusion.

Meanwhile, the good wizard proclaimed to his good people: "Good always conquers evil when it comes right down to it."

Not everyone in the circle was convinced, but they kept thinking positive thoughts. Sure enough, and little by little, the witch's bad spell started to melt away... but not entirely. Evil can take over for a certain time, but not permanently.

The wizard continued to fight off the bad spell. A few moments later, it looked like most of the town was becoming good again. The people who had the bad spell came out of it and started to call the witch names, and stormed out of his cottage, stating that they were never coming back.

The Widow Worthy snapped, "I don't need your stupid potion to feel young! Nobody likes you anymore. Get out of town!"

People finally realized that that the witch was less than no good for trying to impersonate a good wizard.

The wizard's good energy built to its peak, and the witch was frantic. The people in the wee village decided to hunt down the witch. The witch realized that his evil spell was completely gone, and trouble was coming.

It always does.

As the people closed in on his cottage, the witch grabbed a few potions and flew out the cottage chimney! The peoples' heads turned up to the sky as they watched the witch frantically fly south.

Everybody in the small village was happy as they gathered around the wizard. The wizard's advice was: "Don't let looks deceive you and, remember, good always beats evil."

Everybody in the village went back to their old ways, just being happy and getting along.

42

The Way to the Treasure

Marty was a rather lazy boy who lived in the ancient times of brave knights in shining armor. Marty, unfortunately, wasn't very brave. He was full of potential and had dreams just like any other kid, but he wasn't very motivated.

Marty and his family lived in a small village, and Marty dreamed that one day, the family would get out of that village and live in a grand palace, like the one he saw in a book of castles that had beautiful carved lawns and so many rooms he lost count of them.

Marty's parents always told him, "If you want good things to come to you in life, you must do good things for others." Marty was baffled and didn't understand what his parents told him.

His mom said, "Don't you worry, my son. You will soon understand."

Marty didn't give it another thought, but one fine summer day, as he was wandering around the village, he saw someone struggling to walk. Marty approached and realized that he was a very old, crooked gentleman.

Marty asked kindly, "Are you ok, sir?"

The older gentleman replied, "I am hungry, and I'm in need of water."

Marty, feeling sympathy for this hunched over and thin man, took his arm and walked with him towards his home.

Marty asked him what he was doing in this area, and the old man said, "I'm looking to piece together a puzzle."

Marty thought it was best not to ask what he meant. He didn't really care; he was just being polite, as his mother said he should be.

Marty's mother, a wide-eyed hefty woman with a mass of greying curls, welcomed the visitor. She offered him fresh cool water from the well, some delicious stew, piping hot from the boiling pot, a homemade cookie for dessert, and a cozy cot to rest his weary bones. Marty's father, almost as thin as the visitor, smoked his pipe quietly on his stool by the fire.

Hours later and quite refreshed, the gentleman began to take his leave. Filled with gratitude for Marty's thoughtfulness, he turned to Marty's parents on his way out the door and said, "Marty is a blessing in my life. For his good deed, I shall reward him."

With a grand flourish, he handed Marty a crunched up and faded piece of a map. Marty's mother's eyes popped open even wider! Marty, on the other hand, tried to hide his disappointment at such a useless thank you gift.

The older gentleman explained, "There are two other pieces of this map somewhere in this village. If you find them, they will lead you to a bountiful treasure. As many years as I've searched, I was never able to find the missing pieces." He sighed with regret. "Maybe my sins are too great." Bouncing back, he said lightheartedly, "In any case, I am certain the other pieces are in this village. Use this piece to find the next piece of the map. Good luck, lad."

Marty thanked him for the reward and watched the older gentleman stroll away.

Marty's parents exchanged a look that Marty couldn't quite read. His mother told him, "As I always say, if you want good things to come to you in life, you must do good deeds."

At that moment, Marty understood what he must do. He told his parents, "I believe this is the key to making my dreams… our dreams, come true."

The following day, Marty set out on his journey to look for the next piece of the map. Turning the map this way and that, Marty was led to a thick, dark, and scary forest. Although it was hot and humid, he trudged on, determined to find that next piece of the puzzle, and eventually, all of the pieces.

Suddenly, Marty heard a small voice yell, "Help! Somebody, help me!"

He was confused as to where the sound was coming from. He ran down one path and the sound got fainter. He backtracked, and took another, narrower path, looking all around. From above, he heard a frightened cry, "Please help me! I'm stuck in this tree, and I don't know how to get down."

Marty looked up and saw the tear-stained face of the cutest little blonde girl, about eight years old. Marty told her to calm down, not to worry anymore; he would figure out a way to get her down. The little girl, trying to stop crying as best she could, told him, "I lost my rope and now I'm stuck! If you find the rope, then I'll be able to get down."

Marty searched for the rope all around the base of the tree, and, as he stepped back, he tripped on a fallen tree branch, tumbling hard and spraining his ankle. Marty struggled to get up. As he did, he saw the little girl's rope right under the tree branch upon which he'd tripped! He grabbed the rope, limped back to the tree, and threw the rope to the little girl. Catching it on the first try, Marty watched as she slipped quickly down the rope to the ground.

"You must be a tomboy," Marty said, impressed.

Smiling, she said, "I'm just Lizzy."

Her smile faded when she saw Marty sit back down on the ground in pain. As many eight-year-olds do when faced with a challenging situation, Lizzy started rambling! She thanked Marty over and over again for saving her. She told him about how she was wandering away from her family's campground and how, when she heard a scary noise in the bushes, she used her rope to climb the tree in case there was a lion after her (even though there were no lions in their land).

Anyway, the rope had dropped into the bushes, then she'd started crying, and finally, he showed up - "...like a knight in shining armor!" she said, out of breath. "What's your name?" she asked, suddenly shy.

Marty tried to smile through his pain. "Marty."

Lizzy helped Marty walk back to her tent, where her mother was anxiously waiting for her. Her father was in the woods looking for her and her little brother was playing in the creek. Relieved her daughter was safe, she handed Lizzie some bandages to wrap up Marty's ankle. Her mother obviously had great confidence in her!

Wrapped and ready, Marty jumped up. "Thanks for helping me wrap up my ankle. I must get back on my journey."

Lizzy asked Marty, "If you don't mind me asking, what journey? There's nothing but forest here."

Marty showed her the piece of map that he had and told her, "I'm looking for another piece for this map. It's the way to the treasure."

"Oh," she said distractedly. Lizzy started rummaging through her pockets, pulling out rocks, crushed flowers, a slingshot, and a hair ribbon. Marty wondered if she was going to give him a rock until she dug deeper into her pocket and pulled out a crumpled piece of paper.

She handed the paper to Marty. "Since you helped me down from that tree, I want to give a thank you gift." Marty unfolded the wrinkled paper and was amazed to see that it was the second piece of the map puzzle!

"Where did you get this, Lizzy?" She told him she found it in the forest and decided to keep it because it might come in handy someday.

Smiling from ear to ear, Marty said, "Thank you, Lizzy; you have made me so happy!" He kissed her tiny hand!

The little girl blushed, "You're welcome, my shining knight. You deserve it after the good deed you did. Good luck on your journey. I will never forget you."

Once outside, Marty lined up the two pieces of the map and studied the clues. Somehow, something looked very familiar. In fact, he realized the map actually led right back to his own house! How could that be?

Once he arrived home, he told his parents that the last piece of the treasure map must be somewhere around the house. His parents smiled at him. Then his mother walked over to the locked inlaid box she had never opened and unlocked it with the long key that she always wore around her neck. She took out the last piece of the map and handed it to her son.

Marty couldn't believe it. The last and most important piece of the map was here all along. He realized that his parents taught him how to get good things in his life. Being kind to others and doing noble things was the important lesson that he learned. His parents always knew he had the potential for great things, and that was why he was tested to search for the pieces of the map.

When the early sun rose the next day, Marty set out to look for the treasure, carrying a knapsack and a shovel. Following the lines of the map, with the clues, Marty found himself at a cemetery just outside of town. Sure enough, there was the grave marked on the map, "GIVENS FAMILY."

He started to dig. Before too long, the shovel hit something solid, and Marty knew he had found the treasure. He carried the beautiful, crystal studded treasure box back home.

With his parents watching closely, Marty opened the box.

True to the old gentleman's word, the box was filled with a bountiful treasure of beautiful jewels and sparkling gold coins, more wealth than any of them had ever imagined.

His parents were very proud of him, and at that very moment, Marty's dreams started to come true. By the time the first snows of winter fell, the family moved into the palace they had been dreaming of for so long.

Sure enough, there were too many rooms to count!

The End

About the Author

Martin B. Flores was born in Managua, Nicaragua. He and his family migrated to the United States of America in 1988, when he was just six months old. Currently living in Los Angeles, CA, Martin has his Associate Degree in Business Fundamentals from the University of Phoenix. He decided to become an author because he enjoys writing and wants to inspire others with his work. Through his debut book, *10*, Martin aspires to join the ranks of successful Nicaraguan authors while inspiring other migrant writers to do the same.